Nate by Night

Portunus Publishing Company
27875 Berwick Drive, Suite A, Carmel, CA 93923-8518
www.portunus.net

Published by Portunus Publishing Company
27875 Berwick Drive, Suite A
Carmel, CA 93923-8518
Toll Free Orders: 888/450-5021
Fax: 831/622-0681
Web Site: http://www.portunus.net
E-mail: service@portunus.net

Design: Anna Pomaska and David Kirby
Edited by Donna Clark

Publisher's Cataloging-in-Publication
(Provided by Quality Books, Inc.)

Swaim, Jessica
     Nate by Night / by Jessica Swaim ; illustrated
by Helen O'Dea.—1st ed.
     p. cm.
     SUMMARY: Dreaming of success in school, sports,
and music lessons helps young Nate McTate find
ways to make his dreams come true in real life.
     LCCN: 99-67539
     ISBN: 1-886440-02-6 (hc)

     1. Dreams—Juvenile fiction. 2. Self-esteem in
children—Juvenile fiction. I. O'Dea, Helen.
II. Title.

          PZ7.S969893Na 2000   [E]
                    QB199-1629

For Stephen,
Who knows how to fly

Nate McTate looked like an ordinary boy. He had a thick mop of brown hair, deep brown eyes, and a band of freckles across his nose.

He lived in a plain white house with his mother and his father and his wiener dog, Dill Pickle.

By day, Nate lived a normal life.

But at night, in his dreams...

…Nate flew. He left his bed and floated up the chimney, hovering on a breeze. He drifted over the rooftops of his town, spinning all the weather vanes as he passed.

All night long Nate flew.

When the sun came up, he floated back down the chimney and landed in his very own bed.

"Rise and shine, sleepyhead," Nate's mother said every morning. "Don't forget to feed Dill Pickle," his father reminded him. And another day began.

At school, Nate's teacher Ms. Harper asked him to write his name ten times on the blackboard. Nate always got his letters mixed up.

"N-e-a-t spells Neat," Scully Peck sneered. "Take your seat, Neat. And don't trip over your feet." The whole class laughed.

All day, Nate slouched at his desk.

But that night in his dreams...

...Nate wrote his name in the stars, big enough for the whole world to see. It was easy to get it right. All he had to do was connect the dots.

When morning came, his mother said, "Rise and shine sleepyhead." His father reminded him to feed Dill Pickle. And another day began.

At school, Nate went to gym.
"Nate, you're late," said Mr. Sims. "Run." Nate ran three laps around the gym. As usual, he came in last.
The other kids snickered. "What a slowpoke."

Nate hid in the locker room until
Mr. Sims sent him off to class.

But that night...

...Nate soared on Pegasus across the Milky Way. With the wind in his hair, he galloped past Aries, past Ursa, past Taurus the Bull. Rightside up and upside down Nate rode.

Then home he raced on his wild silver steed, down the chimney, into bed.

At recess the next
day, Nate played baseball.
"Look out, sucker!" Scully Peck fired
his fastball toward home plate.
Nate swung. And swung. And swung.
"Strike three!" yelled the umpire.
"You're out!"

Nate slumped in the dugout.

But that night...

...in his dreams, Orion pitched him the moon. Nate swung hard and hit it clear out of the solar system. "Home run!" Orion patted him on the back. "Way to go, Nate."

After nine full innings, down the chimney Nate slid.

As the sun crept over the hills, Nate remembered to feed Dill Pickle without being told. At the bus stop he practiced writing his name in the dust.

N-a-t-e, he printed on the board when he got to school.

"Perfect," said Ms. Harper. And the whole class clapped, even Scully Peck.

After school, Nate went to his swimming lesson.

"Come on in, Nate," said Ms. Flynn. "The water's great."

But Nate shook his head. "No thank you," he told her. He was afraid he would sink to the bottom and never come up.

By day, Nate dangled his feet in the baby pool.

But by night...

…he leaped with the dolphins in the midnight sea. The turtles taught him to paddle. The otters helped him glide on his back.

When the waves washed him home on a clipper ship cloud, Nate sank into his comforter and sighed.

The next day after school, Nate played his recorder.

All that came out was a squeak and a squawk and a sound like a cat choking on a hairball. "Remember, Nate, to concentrate," his mother reminded him.

While Nate practiced, his father groaned on the porch, his mother wore earmuffs, and Dill Pickle howled.

Nate was so frustrated, he kicked over his music stand.

But that night...

…he grabbed the Little Dipper and wailed the blues. His low notes rolled like thunder. His high notes shot fireworks into the sky. Saturn spun. Martians swung to the bippety-bop beat, till morning came.

"Wake up, sleepyhead. Rise and shine."

In gym, Nate dashed across the finish line.

At recess, he hit a line drive that knocked Scully Peck's hat off.

He put his face in the pool and kicked for Ms. Flynn, and he played "Twinkle, Twinkle Little Star" on his recorder without a single mistake.

"I must be dreaming," Nate said. He pinched himself to prove he wasn't.

That night he swooped as silent as an owl over forests,
lakes, and moonlit mountains. Earth, wide and wondrous, was
his to explore. Nate rose high in the sky. He did a somersault
and a couple of loop-de-loops, just because he could.

All night long Nate soared.

When he landed at home, all was quiet. No one else was awake, not even Dill Pickle.

But Nate couldn't wait to start the new day.

He ran into his parents' room and kissed his mother on the cheek.

"Rise and shine, sleepyhead," he said.

And a new day began.

The End